MW00886081

Copyright © 2024 by James W. Johnston, Sr., and Jessica Johnston. Shiloh Publishing House.

All rights reserved. No part of this publication may be reproduced, stored, or transmitted in any form or by any means, electronic, mechanical, photocopying, recording, scanning, or otherwise, without written permission from the publisher. It is illegal to copy this book, post it to a website, or distribute it by any other means without permission.

James W. Johnston Sr., and Jessica Johnston assert the moral right to be identified as the authors of this work.

First edition

In Memory of my grandfather, James Willard Johnston, Sr., lovingly known as Gramps. He is the author of this story that he preached many years ago.
May his memory be blessed in the earth.

My name is Clip Clop and this is my amazing story.

I witnessed the greatest miracle the world has known.
Let me start from the beginning.

I belonged to a man named Reuben of the city of Nazareth. Reuben was a cruel master. He often beat me. I was bigger than the average donkey, so he made me carry heavy loads, loads that I could hardly handle.

One day, he overloaded me with clay water pots. They were so heavy that finally I slipped and fell. The load shifted on my back as I went down and smashed those pots into a thousand pieces. Reuben was furious! He began to beat me. I tried to get up, but my leg hurt so badly that I couldn't stand.

I thought he would surely kill me when all of a sudden, a strong voice said, "Don't hit that donkey another blow!" I looked and saw a man holding Reuben's arm in a tight grip. Reuben was mad!

The stranger said, “Do you want to sell this animal?”
To which Reuben said, “Gladly!” The man named a
price. “Sold” said Reuben, “and good riddance” .

Then, this man bent over me and began to talk to me, and I understood everything he said. “You won’t get anymore beatings from me, lil’fella, but first, let’s look at that leg.”

He took some oil from a pouch on his donkey and began to massage my leg. It hurt at his touch and began to sting and burn. Then, all of a sudden, it began to feel cool.

After a few minutes, he said,
“Let’s see if you can stand” and
immediately I stood.

He took me home with him, and every day, he treated my leg until it felt strong and well. For the first time, as I walked, I noticed that I made a funny sound on the cobblestone streets of Nazereth. It was a definite clip-clop. I guess I had gotten into the habit of putting my weight on my three strong legs and was favoring my injured leg.

One day, I heard Joseph (that was his name) say to me, "Well, big fella, I've been wanting to give you a name. I'm going to call you Clip Clop." So, from that day until now, I was known as Clip Clop.

Then one day I met Mary. She was a beautiful lady and I know she must be someone special because of the way Joseph looked at her.

Joseph would ride me to Mary's house, then he would put Mary on my back and walk us out into the countryside.

Then they would walk hand in hand across the meadows, running and playing and laughing like children. I knew they loved each other.

Then one day Mary told Joseph something that upset
Joseph. She told Joseph that an angel had visited her
and told her that God had chosen her to be the mother
of the long-awaited Messiah.

I had heard the people of Nazareth speak of the coming of a Messiah who would be the King of the Jews. Most people looked forward to this event, but Reuben. He used to say "Poppycock! That's just a bunch of old wives' tales."

And now he was to come and Mary would be the mother of this Messiah who would be called Jesus! Joseph couldn't understand all that Mary was saying to him. He took her back to the city and he told her goodbye.

When we left, I could see the tears in his eyes. Joseph was hurt. He began to talk to me. “Why would she do this to me, Clip Clop?” I’ve been true to her and she says she’s been true to me, but how could she have a baby.”

He was so hurt. I wanted to sympathize with him, but you know, we animals can't talk, so I just lowered my head and carried him gently as I could across the cobblestone streets of Nazareth. I hardly slept all night. Joseph kept his light on in his room till early in the morning. Then it went out, and I tried to get some sleep.

Early the next morning he was up and seemed very excited. “Clip Clop, it's all right! I just talked to an angel last night, and he said, ‘Don't be afraid to take Mary as your wife' “ He got on my back and we really took off.

In just a few minutes we were at Mary's house. He knocked on her door, and when she came to the door he said a few words and then she was in his arms. Such hugging I've never seen!

In just a few days, Mary came to live with Joseph, and they lived together as husband and wife. The next few months were happy months, and all the animals were aware of this happiness.

Then one day Joseph told Mary that the Emperor of Rome, Caesar Augustus, had issued a decree that everyone must go to his birthplace to register for the census and pay his taxes.

Joseph said, "We have got to go to Bethlehem, but I fear the trip will be too much for you. You are due to have the baby any day now." Mary said, "It's all right, Joseph. It's God's will that we go, and He will watch out for me. He will take care of me."

The day came for the trip. Joseph said to me "Clip Clop, I want you to carry Mary, and I'm counting on you to carry her as easily as you can."

I understood every word he said.

We started out with Mary on my back and Joseph leading the way. The road was rough with many hills and grades. It was dusty, and we often had to move off the highways when the Roman soldiers came by on their chariots.

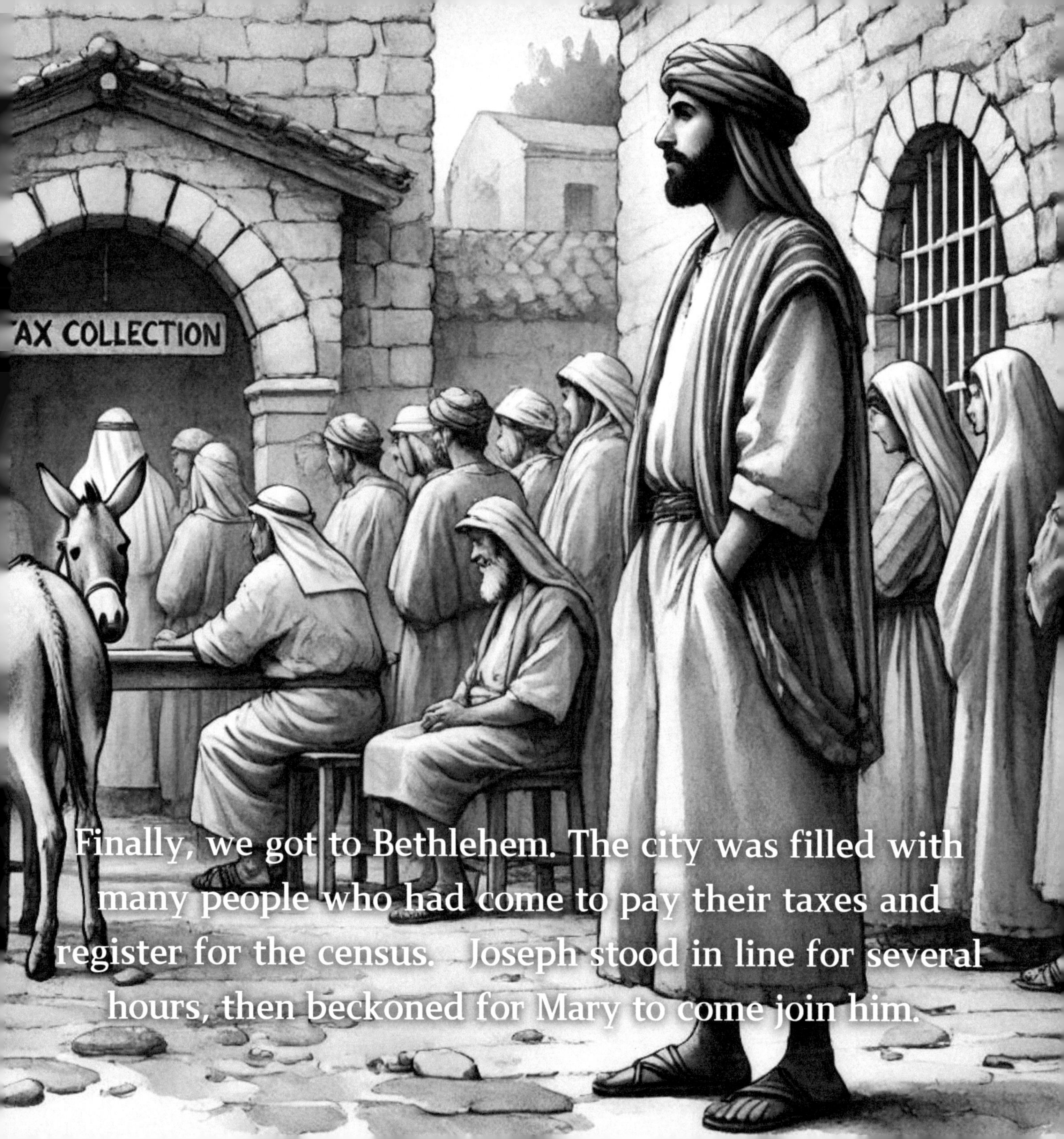

Finally, we got to Bethlehem. The city was filled with many people who had come to pay their taxes and register for the census. Joseph stood in line for several hours, then beckoned for Mary to come join him.

After the registration, they looked for an Inn in which to spend the night. Whenever Joseph asked for lodging, he was told, "There's no room."

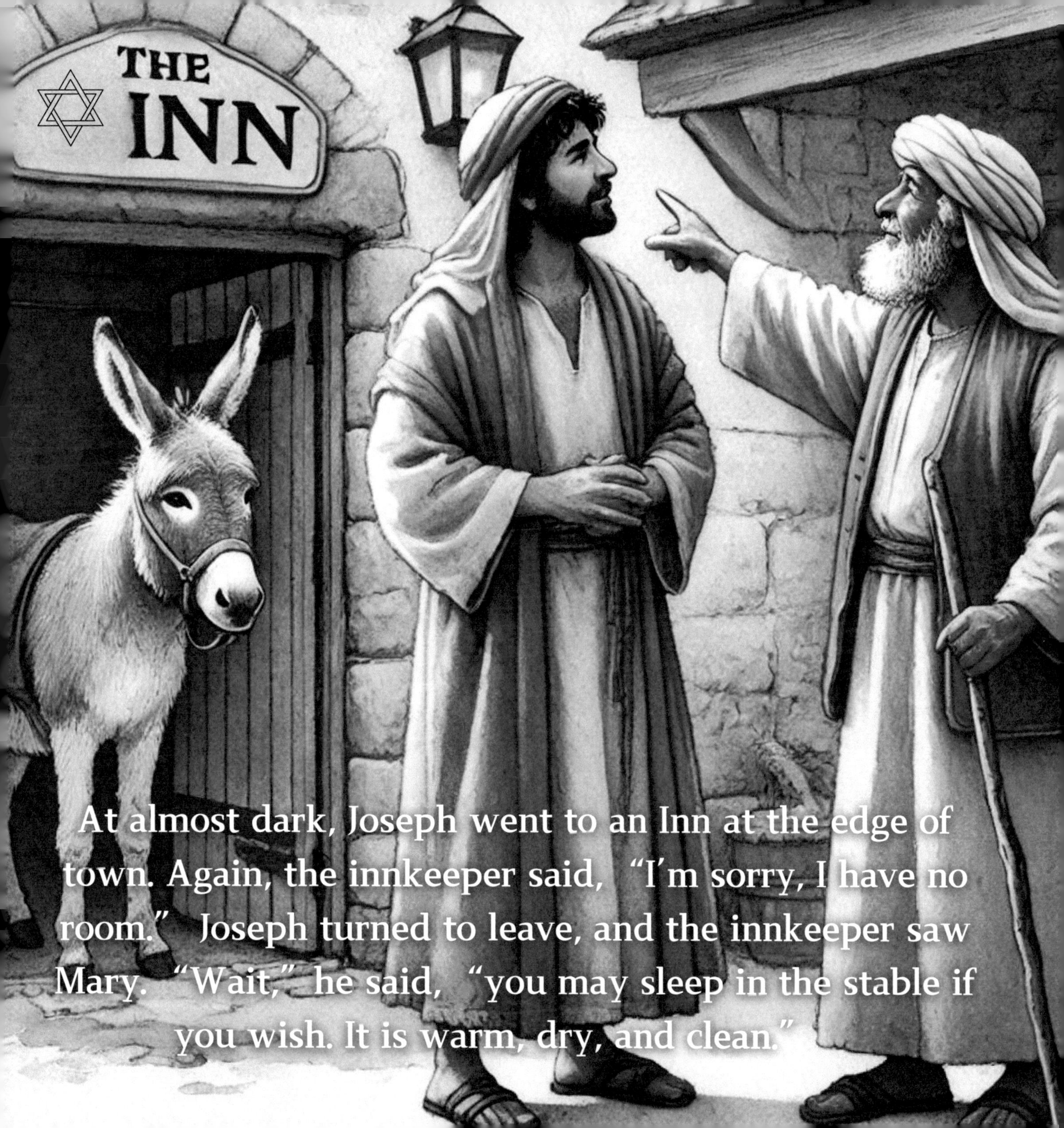

At almost dark, Joseph went to an Inn at the edge of town. Again, the innkeeper said, “I’m sorry, I have no room.” Joseph turned to leave, and the innkeeper saw Mary. “Wait,” he said, “you may sleep in the stable if you wish. It is warm, dry, and clean.”

Joseph thanked him, and we found our way to the stable. It was indeed, warm, dry, and clean. Joseph made a bed for Mary and then brought water and fresh hay for me. I could see that he was tired but relieved that we all had a warm place to stay.

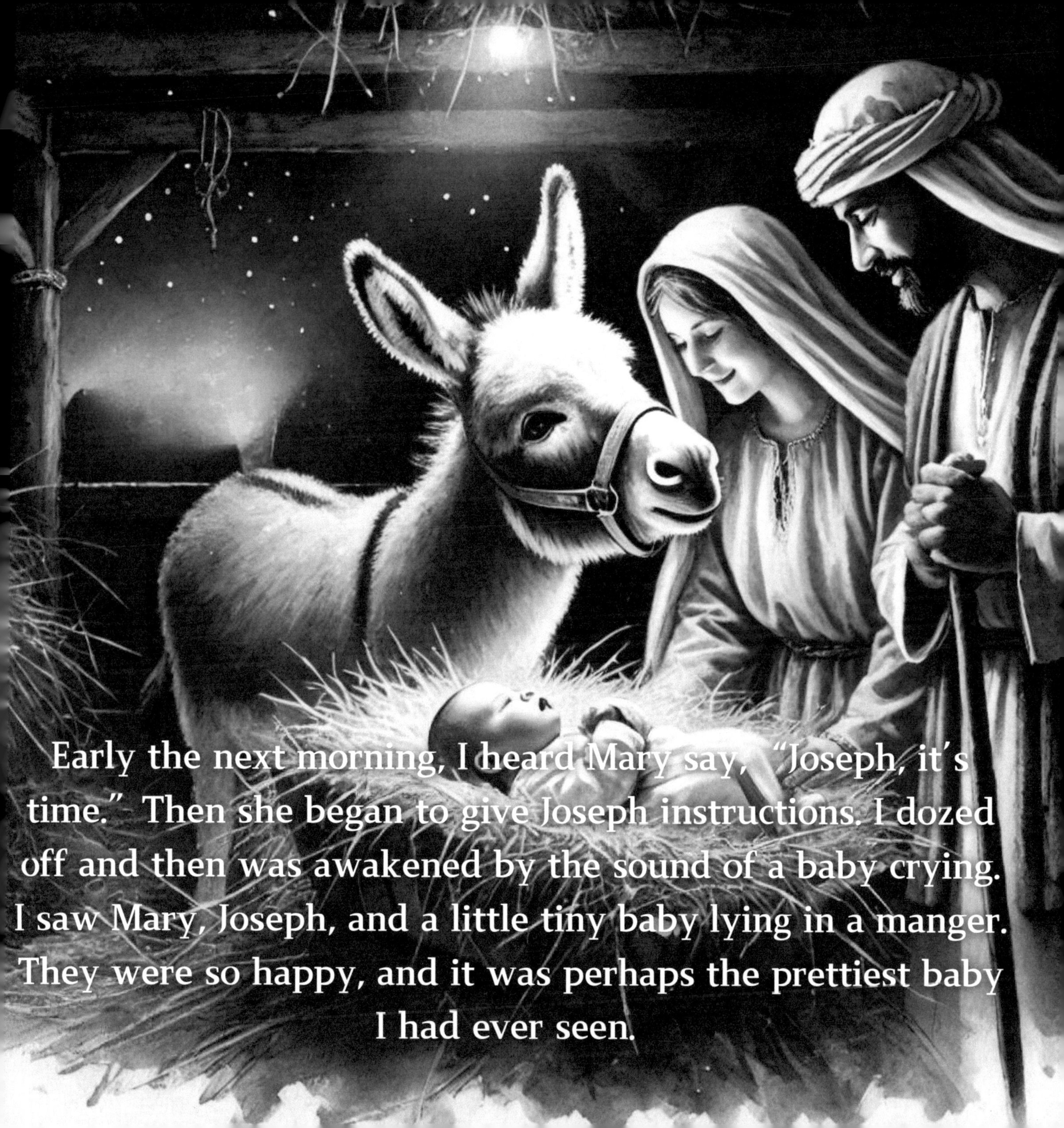

Early the next morning, I heard Mary say, "Joseph, it's time." Then she began to give Joseph instructions. I dozed off and then was awakened by the sound of a baby crying. I saw Mary, Joseph, and a little tiny baby lying in a manger. They were so happy, and it was perhaps the prettiest baby I had ever seen.

Shortly afterwards some shepherds came and said an angel had visited them in the fields. The angel told them to come to Bethlehem and find the baby Jesus lying in a manger.

Mary showed them the baby and they fell down and worshipped. For the first time I realized this was the long-awaited Messiah that the world had been waiting for.

Then I did a very strange thing. I walked over to baby Jesus and knelt down before him, bent over him, and licked his face with my tongue.
Clip Clop had met the Messiah.

A Note from the Author

I hope you enjoyed this story about Clip Clop, the Bethlehem Donkey. It is the true story of Jesus' birth with some imagination thrown in from my grandfather about the donkey that carried Mary and witnessed this miracle. My grandfather wrote this as a sermon. He was a great storyteller.

If you enjoyed this book, please consider leaving us an honest review on Amazon. You can also follow me there on the book page for information on more books to come. Thank you, and happy reading!

Jessica Johnston

Made in United States
Cleveland, OH
16 December 2024